Trust

BY ELIZABETH HOLCOMBE

Dorrance Publishing Co
585 Alpha Drive
Pittsburgh, PA 15238
Visit our website at *www.dorrancebookstore.com*

ISBN: 978-1-4809-2002-6
eISBN: 978-1-4809-2117-7

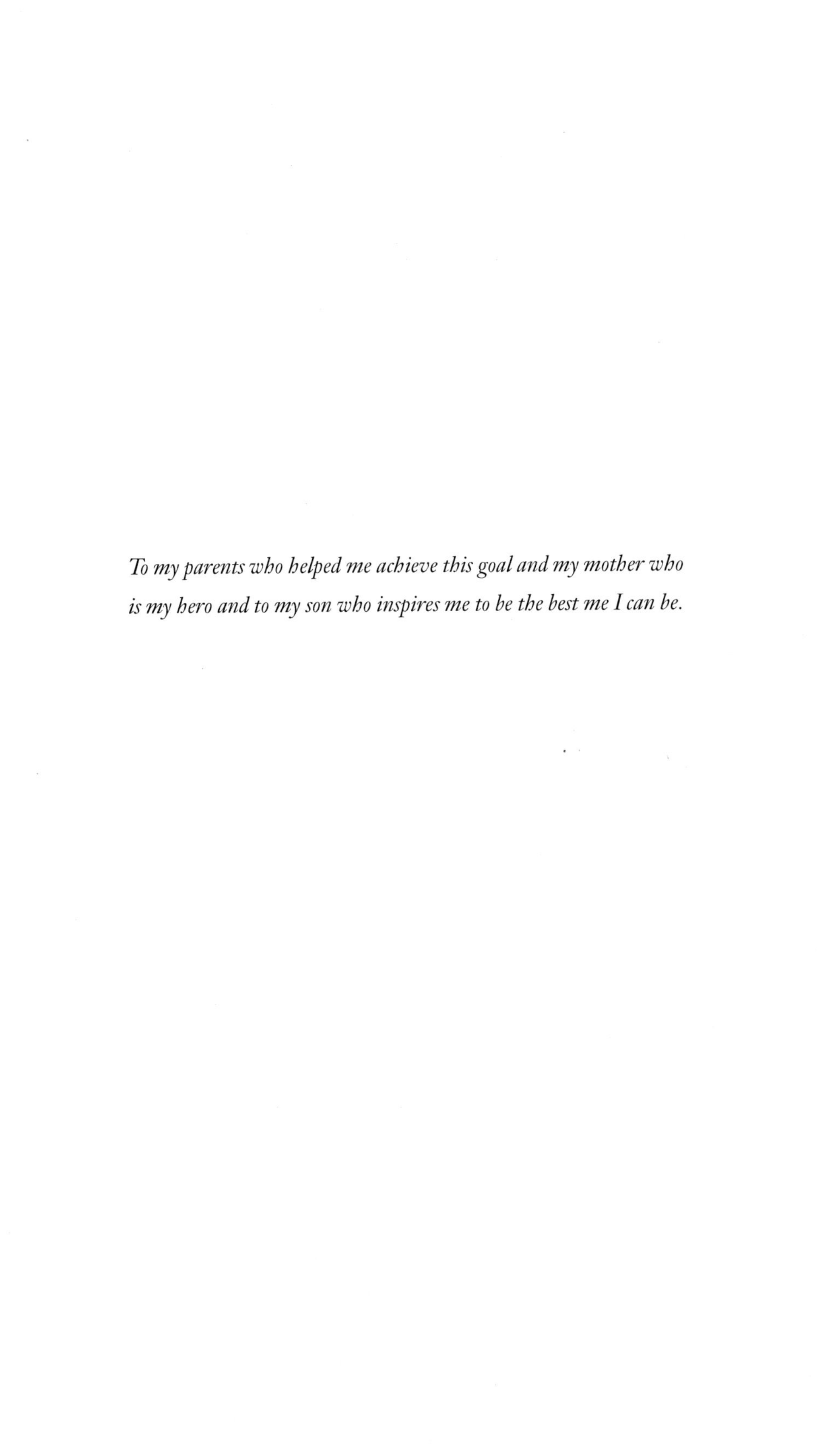

To my parents who helped me achieve this goal and my mother who is my hero and to my son who inspires me to be the best me I can be.

Chapter One

New Town, Same Old Results

Life. It has a crazy way of changing on us. Becoming friends with people who only want to use us, falling in love with someone our parents may not like, having our heart broken, and even getting hurt by our family. Who can we trust with our heart? When can we expect not to be hurt? Even in fairytales, someone gets hurt. You hardly ever meet someone who won't hurt you. It only happens once, and not everyone gets to experience that once-in-a-lifetime kind of love. It happened for me when I almost gave up hope. I found someone who didn't hurt me, who made me smile without trying. I fell in love with the most imperfect guy.

I guess I should start from the beginning, if I'm going to tell you about a once-in-a-lifetime experience that I was lucky to have. It wasn't an easy journey to this happy life I'm now living. My story begins in a new town with new people six months before my eighteenth birthday.

"Denise, sweetheart, cheer up. It won't be so bad," my mother said in the car on the drive to our new house.

My dad left us, and my mom couldn't take living in the same state. She dragged me away from my friends, my home, and my family. Why did we have to move? He was the one who left us, so shouldn't he be the one who should move?

I used to live in Dayton, Ohio, a very boring town and state. We moved to Evansville, Indiana, another boring town and state. The only upside about living there was that we would be closer to family we rarely saw.

"Mom, we lived off of your old job and you don't really have a job now, so how are we going to live?"

"Denise, we will be okay, I promise. Yes, money is going to be a little tight, but we've got each other."

My mother has been saying that ever since Dad left. She used to say it before he came into our lives and while she had a crappy job. I guess that's why she and I are so close. We really have had each other through all our troubles. Now, all of you are probably still caught up on the "before Dad" statement. Yes, before my dad became a part of my life, but don't worry, I'll explain later. So let's get back to the story.

After I heard my mother say that, all I could do was look out the window, see our new house, and go find my new room. The walls are painted dark blue, just the same as the old house. I sat on my bed and look at the boxes against the walls, wondering which one has my sheets and my pictures. I saw my bookshelves and decided to unpack all of my books. After I unpacked a few boxes, I decided I need to get out of the house.

"Mom, I'm going for a walk. I'll be back before dinner."

"Denise, take your cell phone, please, and how does Chinese sound for dinner?"

"Sounds good, Mom," I said while walking out the door.

As I stepped outside, I felt the sun's heat as it set against my flesh. I took a look around and decided to head to what appeared to be an empty park down the street. When I arrived at the park, though, I saw a little girl with her dad pushing her on the swing. The little girl's mother was on the other side of her, smiling while holding her stomach. While watching this happy family, I began to have a flashback to my childhood, something I tried to block out.

"Mommy, Mommy, where's Daddy?" I used to ask.

She would always have to remind me that he only visited me every Saturday. I was always trying to be Daddy's little girl. Even though he was hardly ever there, I still wanted to be his little girl, at least while I was really young. I realized as I got older that I could never be as close to him as I was to my mother.

As I started to come back to reality, the happy family was leaving. While they were leaving, I glided over to the swings. As I was swinging through the air, I began to relax and close my eyes. By the time I opened my eyes again, I saw stars in the sky and decided I better head home.

"It's not smart to be out this late at night," a young man spoke softly.

I decided the best thing to do was ignore him after I realized he was roughly the same age as me. I went around and started toward my house, thinking he would leave me be.

"Wait!" he yelled. "Let me walk you home. My name's Ethan, and I'm guessing you're new around here."

Why couldn't this guy leave me alone?

"So, what's your name?" he asked after I didn't respond.

"Denise," I mumbled.

"That's a pretty name. So are you going to college or are you still in high school?"

"I'm going to be a senior in high school...."

"So am I. What high school are you attending?"

"Central High School. Why do you care?"

"Well, I don't know, you just seemed like you needed a friend. By the way, you are attending the same school as me. We might just be classmates, so why not become friends before school starts? It'll help your first day to have at least one person, right?" He smiled.

I had stopped walking to look at him and because I was in front of my house.

"Well, thanks, but I don't think you really want to be friends with me, so goodbye," I said, then walked in my house, not waiting for a response.

When I closed the door, I smelled dinner. My mom and I ate in silence for the first time since Dad left. After we finished cleaning up, I headed upstairs to my new room. As I turned off the lights and fell back on my bed, I curled up in a ball. I began to feel my eyes get wet and my vision blurred with tears. I missed my friends, and as much as I hated to admit it I also missed being a family of three. It angered me so much that I missed the man who hurt my mom and me. I let the tears flow knowing that no one was around to see them. I hoped the next day would be a little easier. And so, that night—my first in a new town—I cried myself to sleep. New town, same old results.

Chapter Two

THAT BOY

I woke up to the smell of pancakes, knowing my mom would have had to get up to run to the store in order to make them. While I dragged myself down the stairs, I heard my mother talking to someone. I cautiously rounded the corner to my kitchen, and I saw my mom sitting at the table with a boy who looked familiar. Sure enough, it was the talkative boy from last night. I tried to sneak back upstairs, but my mother spotted me.

"Morning, Denise. How did you sleep? I made pancakes," she rambled on as I sat on the opposite side of the table from our guest.

"I slept fine. What's with having a guest this early in the morning?"

"Well, sweetie, he was out walking this morning and the car stopped a mile down the street, and he helped get the car working again. Anyway, I asked if he could tell me where the closest grocery was, and he tried to give me directions, but you know me. So he went with me, and then I asked him to stay for breakfast as a thank-you for helping me."

"Why didn't you wake me up so I didn't have to come down in my pajamas? Or at all!" I said, the last part in a whisper, knowing my mom wouldn't hear me.

"That's my fault. I told your mother we met last night and not to worry about waking you," said the boy. "Oh, by the way, you forgot, my name is Ethan."

"I didn't forget your name."

I had forgotten his name.

"So what are you up to today? Need help unpacking? Maybe I could show you around, since you're new and all."

"Mom, will you excuse us? We will be upstairs. I still have a few things to unpack."

"Okay, sweetheart. I'm going to go look for a job, be back in a few hours," my mother said while grabbing her purse.

I didn't wait for him to follow. I just headed up the stairs. When I got to my room, I stopped, turned around, and glared into Ethan's bright blue eyes.

"What do you want? Did you not get the hint last night? Leave me alone! Please!" I screamed before falling on my bed and hiding my face in my hands.

Instead of leaving me, he sat next to me on my bed. "Everyone needs a friend, and I'm not going away until you give me the chance to be friends with you." He smiled.

I sighed and looked up in his big blue eyes, which I had tried glaring at. "Okay, do you really want to help me unpack, though?" I asked while standing.

"Not really. I'd rather show you around the town."

"Do you have a car?"

"Yes. Why do you want to know?"

"Would you let me drive it to CHS and then you can take me any place you want to?" I said while pushing him out the bedroom door. As I went to shut the door, he looked at me with a very confused face. "I can't get dressed with you in my room." I smiled and closed the door.

I ran down the stairs in cutoff shorts and a black tank top. I wasn't expecting Ethan to be standing at the last step and ran into him, knocking us both to the ground. I realized I had fallen on him and scrambled up, mumbling an apology. Grabbing my phone and slipping on my flip-flops, I led the way out the door.

On the way to his house, he started to ask me questions, probably to make the time fly by faster. "So where are you from?" he asked.

"Well, we moved here from Ohio."

"Did you move close to CHS for its reviews or family?"

"Yes and no. My mom hadn't planned on moving, but a month before I ended my junior year, my dad left us. My mom was in so much pain. She needed me and family, so I started looking for schools close to family and told my mom. She told me she wouldn't take me away for my senior year, but I told her it would all work out. Then she moved us both out here."

"I'm sorry about your dad. How are you holding up?'

"I'm okay. I learned a long time ago you can't trust anyone with your feelings."

I was beginning to open up, and I didn't know why. I didn't like talking about myself. Normally, I could avoid questions that involved my personal life. Being friends with Ethan could turn out to be a bad idea and would hurt because everyone disappoints.

We finally arrived at his house, and a little girl was playing in the yard. She looked up and ran to hug Ethan. She had big blue eyes and big brown curls, just like him. As I looked at Ethan holding this little girl, I saw something precious. Something that caused me to feel as if I needed to get away from him. I knew I might start to open up to him, which scared me and made me want to run. At the same time, I didn't want to leave his side.

"Carly, this is Denise. Denise, this is my little sister, Carly."

"Hi, Carly. That is a pretty dress you have on."

"Thank you." She smiled shyly.

I knelt down in front of her. "How old are you, Carly?"

"I'm five!" She giggled.

"Are you going to be starting kindergarten?"

"Yep! I'm going to be in school, just like Bubby."

"That's cool. What's your favorite color?"

"Purple." She smiled. "Denise, do you want to play with me?"

"Carly, Denise and I are leaving soon," Ethan interjected. "I need to talk to Dad. Is he in the house?"

"I can stay out here and play with her until you get back," I said.

Ethan looked at me and nodded before heading into his house.

Twenty minutes later, Ethan and an older man walked to where Carly and I were sitting. I stood up and so did Carly. Ethan looked as if he wanted to grab me and leave as fast as we could run.

"Hello, my name is Will. I'm Carly and Ethan's father. You must be new to the neighborhood," said Ethan's father with a smile that seemed to be forced.

"Hello, sir. My name is Denise and, yes, my mother and I just moved here." I was still pondering the look Ethan had when he walked out with this man.

"Ethan here says you two want to head down to the high school. Mind if I ask why you want to go to the school during summer?"

"Well, I just wanted to know how to get there from my house."

"Oh, okay. Well, do you mind if Carly goes with you two? I need to run over to a friend's house tonight, and Carly can't be left alone or go with me."

"I don't mind, sir," I said as Ethan walked over, picking up Carly's toys.

His dad took the toys from Ethan, handed him car keys, and then walked inside. I walked over to Carly, picked her up, and then followed Ethan to the car. He had a blue Explorer. I helped Carly into her seat in the back and turned around to see Ethan holding the door open for me. After we all were buckled in, we started toward CHS.

"Bubby, can we listen to Taylor Swift's disk, please?" Carly asked.

Ethan pressed the play button and turned the volume up. The first song to play was "Fifteen." I was getting ready to ask to change the song, but Carly was singing to it, so I looked out the window, preparing myself for the flashback that I always got no matter how much I tried to block it out when listening to that song.

"I hate you! You lied to me! Who lies about their child's father! Who he is? Who lies about that?" I yelled at my mother during the beginning of my eighth-grade year.

That summer I learned more than my eighth-grade mind could handle. My dad wasn't who we thought he was. Plus, I met my real dad, and my mom started dating.

I felt tears slide down my cheek but quickly wiped them away before Ethan could see them, wishing at the same time to understand why that song always triggered that particular memory.

As we pulled into the school's parking lot, "Love Story" started to play. I smiled, knowing that was my mom's favorite song and how many times we listened to it on the way to our new home.

"Denise, will you help Carly out of her seat in the back?" Ethan asked.

"No problem. Are you okay?"

"I'm fine. Just disagreement between Dad and me, that's all."

We all walked up to the school's doors and walked in, and as we started making our way around, Carly walked over and held my hand. I looked back to see Ethan smiling at us. I soon felt Carly tugging on my hand.

"Yes, Carly?"

"Denise, will you pick me up and carry me, please?"

I looked down and saw her smiling up at me. I laughed to myself and bent down to pick her up. After I had Carly in my arms, I slowed down to talk to Ethan.

"So, what is your favorite part about Central High School?"

"I like our history teachers. That's what I'm going to be going to college for next year, to become a history professor," he said.

"Wow, that's really cool."

"What are you looking forward to, and what are your plans for the future?"

"I want to be an English teacher. I decided that a long time ago, when I first fell in love with reading literature. I guess what I'm looking forward to about coming here, though, would have to be starting over."

"What do you mean by starting over?"

"No one here knows me, so I hope to be able to keep everything to myself about my life. Back home everyone knows too much about me and treated me differently because of that. Everyone's goal back home was to make the girl who trusts no one to open up and trust."

When I stopped walking, Ethan looked at me. We had walked all around campus, and Carly had fallen asleep in my arms.

"Maybe we should head back to the car."

"I can carry her, if you would like me to."

"No, it's okay. She's not heavy. Besides, it doesn't really bother me." I smiled at him.

I climbed in the passenger seat and looked at Ethan as he started the car. The more I looked at Ethan, the more I wanted to run. The more I felt myself becoming closer to him, which was what I had taught myself to fight against for so long. Something about his smile and the way he looked at me holding his sister scared me. I might open myself up to him and trust him—the one thing I'd never done before. I didn't know if I even knew how to trust. I was not a big fan of new experiences, and Ethan was a new experience. I needed to get away. I could never be friends with that boy.

Chapter Three

Running

The next morning, I woke to my cell phone ringing. When I looked at my phone, I saw Ethan's name. He had sent me a text asking what my plans were for the day and if I would like to hang out with him. I ignored his question as a way to put space between us, got up, got dressed, and finished unpacking my room. Once my room was organized, I went downstairs to see my mom sitting at the kitchen table, filling out applications.

"Morning, Mom. Need any help dropping off the finished ones?" I asked.

"Oh, no, sweetheart. You don't want to spend the day helping me. Why don't you spend your day with Ethan? He seems like a nice guy, maybe even a future boyfriend?"

"I don't want a boyfriend, and I don't want to waste my time getting to know someone who is going to hurt me or leave my life for a stupid reason."

"Denise, you can't keep pushing people away. Not everyone is going to hurt you. I'm sorry you've had a shitty life and that I haven't helped keep you from getting hurt, but that doesn't mean everyone is going to hurt you."

"You don't know that! Look at our life now. Look at what happened in my past! Opening up to people allows them to be able to hurt you by gaining and destroying your trust. I'm going for a walk!"

I stormed out the door. I walked in the opposite direction of Ethan's house. I wanted to run, and lucky for me, I had tennis shoes on.

I began to run, not knowing or caring where I would end up. I ran up to the first traffic light and turned the corner. I ran past people and cars, refusing to stop. I was running faster and faster until I ran into someone. I went to apologize and saw it was Ethan. I got up and started running again. I heard him yelling my name, but I didn't stop or look back. I saw an alley up ahead and pushed myself to run faster to turn into the alley. I went to hide next to some crates, hoping Ethan didn't follow me down the alley. I curled myself into a ball and placed my head on my knees. Knowing now that I was alone, I began crying softly. I was hurt because I hated fighting with my mom. I also hated people seeing me upset. More than any of those things, I hated getting close to people.

I was starting to fall asleep against the wall and figured I should start heading home. I opened my eyes and heard a loud crash toward the exit of the alley. I looked around the crate and saw two men who appeared to be drunk. I looked at my phone and saw that I had no service. The crate was big enough for one to hide under, so I slid between the wall and the crate, hoping they would leave. I heard them getting closer. I couldn't breathe. The men were outside of my hiding spot. They started to look around and throw the cans they just finished in the dumpster beside me. I wanted to close my eyes, but I couldn't get them to close. I saw one man stop right in front of the crate. I moved slightly, and my phone found one bar of service and went off. My mom was calling. The men moved the crate, and I put the phone on speaker in my pocket so my mom would hear that I was in trouble.

"Hey, sexy. What's a pretty little thing like you doing down here?" the taller man asked.

I didn't respond. I was seeing if I would be able to make a run for it without them catching or stopping me. I didn't know much self-defense, and I didn't want to fight because I knew I would lose to two grown men. As I was thinking of my escape plan, the bigger man caught me off guard and grabbed me. Before I could scream, his filthy hand was over my mouth. The man held me tight as the other man walked toward me. I tried to squirm out of the arms that felt like chains around me. The more I moved, the tighter the chains got.

I hadn't realized where I ran to. I didn't know this part of town or this town at all. I was afraid and didn't know what to do.

"Shh...we just want you to join our party," smiled the taller man as he stroked my cheek.

All I could do was glare and try to fight against the pain of the other guy's arms around me.

"Well, Peter, think we should just party here? No one around, and I don't think I can wait."

"Sure, Ale. I'll keep watch just in case," Peter said while pushing me against Ale.

When I saw the look in his eyes, I was struck with fear. I couldn't get my body to move and fight or my voice to scream. The only thing that was screaming was my mind telling me to run, to not let it happen again, but I couldn't. All I could do was remember what happened when I was a little girl and knew that if it did happen again, this time would be ten times worse. I was frozen with fear.

They knocked me to the ground.

"Ready to party, baby?" asked Ale.

I felt his hand rip my shirt apart. He went to unbutton my jeans, and that was when my mind kicked in, realizing this was really going to happen. I began thrashing against him, but his grip tightened around my arms, pushing me back hard to the ground. I tried kicking with my legs, but soon he was on top of my body. I began to cry, knowing it would be too late if help came. As I felt him slide on me to push my jeans off, I heard a big crash again.

"Pete? Was that you, dude?" Ale asked while still looking at me.

No response, at least not from Peter.

"Denise? Where are you?"

"I'm down here!" I shouted before Ale could cover my mouth. I tried to squirm and make enough noise for someone to find me.

Ale tightened his grip, causing me pain all over, and I felt myself blacking out. Before my eyes closed shut, the pressure on my body released and Ethan's face entered my view. Suddenly everything went black.

Chapter Four

Silenced

When my eyes opened, I was in a too bright of a room with plain white walls. I heard a beeping and saw an IV in my arm. I felt like I was living out a scene in my favorite book, *Twilight*. I saw my mother in the chair next to me, sleeping. With the hand that didn't have a needle in it, I reached up and felt my head. I felt the stitches in the back of my head, understanding why my head was throbbing. I could also see some bruises and could feel the ones I couldn't see. I was thinking of waking my mom up so she could see I was awake, but then someone walked into the room.

"Don't wake her yet. I want to talk to you, if that's okay," said Ethan while sitting in the chair on the other side of my bed. "Denise, why were you down that alley? Why did you run from me?"

"I was scared."

"Of what? Were you afraid of me?"

"Yes and no. I was afraid of my feelings. That I might develop feelings for you, and I can't let that happen. My mom suggested it as well, and I got so upset that I just ran."

"Why would you be afraid of developing feelings for me? If it's because you're afraid I won't return those feelings, I will. I have feelings for you, Denise."

"Please don't say that. We can only be friends. If we ever became a couple, you would end up leaving and hurting me in the end. I am taking a risk by being your friend."

"I wouldn't hurt you. I'll always be here for you. If we don't work as a couple, I'll still always be there for you, I promi—"

"Don't! Don't promise me that you won't leave or hurt me. That's one promise no one can keep."

"I don't want to stress you out while you are still recovering, but at the same time I'm not going to give up on you and I'm not going anywhere. I will see you tomorrow. I know your mom is going to want to talk with you; she was really worried about you," was the last thing he said to me before walking out the door.

I look over at my mom as she began to sit up and stretch. "Hey, sleepyhead," I said to her.

She looked up at me and looked as if she was about to cry. "Denise, sweetheart, are you really awake?"

"Yes, Mom, I'm really awake."

"Oh, Denise!" She started to cry while hugging me without hurting me. "Have you seen Ethan yet? He and I were so worried about you. He is the one who found you and called the police, you know."

"I know, Mom. I saw Ethan before I passed out. I knew you would call him to find me when I put the phone on speaker."

"Sweetheart, why did you run? How did you even end up down there?"

"I ran because I was sick of the pressure from you, so I thought running would clear my head. Then I ran into Ethan and I panicked, so I went down the alley to hide. When I was getting ready to leave, two men came down the alley, so I stayed hidden with no service. I moved slightly and my phone caught service and you were calling, so I made it so you could get me help."

"Why won't you open up and let people in your life anymore?"

"I won't let people in because I can't trust people, Mom. I've been hurt and I've watched you get hurt. People get close to each other, then someone breaks that trust that we develop between each other."

She had nothing to say about that. I don't know if it was that she was shocked by how I felt or if she knew my words were true and didn't know what she could do to change my mind. My mother went to find a doctor, so I closed my eyes, hoping to go home soon.

The next day was the day I got to leave the hospital. Unfortunately my mom had to work, so Ethan came to pick me up. I climbed into his Explorer, and we headed home in silence.

When I couldn't handle how quiet it was, I decided to be the first one to speak. "So how is Carly?" It felt like a safe topic.

"She's fine. She misses you a lot."

"We could stop by your house and I could see her."

"I don't think that is such a great idea with you just getting out of the hospital and all."

"Well, how about we pick Carly up and head over to my house, then? I'll make lunch for the three of us, and you and I can talk."

"I guess. It'll get Carly out of the house for a while, too."

I felt like he intended something different than just getting her out of the house. I couldn't understand why I felt that way or where I had felt that feeling before.

When we pulled up in front of Ethan's house, Carly was in the yard playing tea party. I went to get out and say hi to Carly, but Ethan told me to stay in the car. At first I thought he was being silly over my bruises, and then I saw why he wanted me to stay in the car. Ethan's father came storming out of the house and started yelling at Carly to get her butt inside and to clean the mess she had left. Carly looked terrified and ran in a curve path around her father into the house. After Carly was out of the scene, I realized their father was holding a beer bottle.

Ethan started talking to his dad, who didn't look happy. Then Ethan said something that caused his dad to look up at me. What I saw scared me. His eyes were full of anger. I couldn't help but look away and pray that Ethan and Carly would be in the car soon.

When I heard the door open, it was Ethan helping Carly into the back seat before getting in the driver's seat. I was lost for words to say to Ethan. I felt as if I had been placed into a world that had been silenced.

Chapter Five

STRUGGLE

When I unlocked the door to my house, sounds enveloped us. My stereo was playing loudly. I ran over to the stereo and turned it off.

"Sorry about that. My mother must have been in a hurry when she left. So what would you all like for lunch?"

"I want hot dogs and macaroni and cheese!" Carly spoke up.

"Sounds good. I'll go get started on lunch, and if you want you can go watch TV or color, Carly. The coloring books and supplies are on the bookshelf."

Carly headed toward the living room while Ethan followed me into the kitchen.

"Want some help?" he asked.

"No thanks," I said while placing a pot of water on the stove. "Ethan, I'm sorry about yesterday, the way I acted. I'm trying to open up, but I'm not ready for any relationships besides friendship. I'm also sorry about your dad. You don't have to tell me anything about it, but if you do want to talk I'm here for you."

"Well, don't worry too much about my dad, and thanks for trying to open up to a friendship. Oh, and don't worry about yesterday. We both were a little tired and upset."

I smiled at him as I started to cut the hotdogs into bite size for the macaroni.

We all sat down for lunch, where Carly told me all about her day yesterday at the park. I laughed at how energetic she was and remembered why I loved little kids.

After lunch Ethan helped me get an old board game down from the hall closet, and we all sat and played "Sorry." We ended up playing four rounds, Carly always being the winner.

"I won again!" she yelled while standing on the chair. "You two are really bad at this game. You both can't even beat a five-year-old."

"Oh? I thought we just let her win, right, Ethan?" I said.

"Yes, we did. Sorry, Carly. Denise and I planned this from the very beginning," replied Ethan.

The look on Carly's face was of complete shock. Ethan and I just laughed. I felt bad when Carly sat down and began to pout.

"Carly, we were kidding around. Smile. You really did win." I smiled.

"I don't want to smile," she pouted.

"Well, then I guess you'll just have to get a visit from the tickle monster!" I said as I went to tickle her.

She squirmed away and ran out of the room screaming. Ethan and I just chuckled.

"You are really good with her, you know. Do you have a lot of experience working with younger children?" he asked.

"Not really. I used to babysit, but I worked well with kids before that. I guess it's just something I'm a natural at."

"You'll be a great mother someday."

"Well, uhm, thanks."

After that conversation, the room went quiet and had a very awkward feeling to it. It didn't last long, though, for a few minutes later Carly came rushing back into the kitchen and just stared at us.

"Aww, man!" She smiled. "I thought I would catch you two kissing."

My face turned bright red, and Ethan got up to run after Carly.

For the next few hours, we all watched movies, walked to the park, and played games. It had been the best day I had had for a long time. I was shocked to see my mother walk through the door while Ethan and Carly were still over.

"Hey, kids, what are you all up to?" my mother asked.

"Just playing games, Mom. I didn't realize how late it is. I'll go get dinner started, sorry," I responded.

"Denise, don't worry. I'm going to make dinner. I hope you took it easy today, being that you just got out of the hospital. Would you two like to stay for dinner?" she asked Ethan and Carly, even though I was pretty sure she had no clue who Carly was.

"I'll call our dad and make sure it's okay with him. Thank you," Ethan replied as my mom turned toward the kitchen.

I got up and followed my mom so that Ethan could call his dad without me standing there.

"Who's the little girl?" my mother asked without turning around.

"It's Ethan's little sister, Carly. How was work?"

"It was good. My boss likes me and thinks I might be working on the wrong floor. I might be his new secretary."

"That's amazing, Mom! First day on the job and you already are getting promotions."

"I know it's crazy, but if I get this job we might be back the way we were. Maybe even get you a car so you don't have to take a bus everywhere."

"Wow, you mean that?"

"Yes, I do." She smiled up at me. "Go see if Ethan and Carly are staying for dinner."

I left the kitchen to see Ethan getting off the phone. When he saw me, he nodded and told Carly they would be staying for dinner. About ten minutes later, my mother called us all into sit for dinner.

We all sat and ate and talked. Carly mostly talked to my mom about how we all spent our day. Soon it was time for them to go home, so I walked them out to the car. After Ethan had Carly into the car, he turned and gave me a hug and thanked me for the day. As his car pulled away, I realized being friends with Ethan might not be a struggle.

Chapter Six

SUMMER

Over the next two months, Ethan, Carly, and I spent many days together. We went to the park, went to the movies, even played tea party with Carly. For once I wasn't afraid. I felt as if I had trustworthy friends, almost. It was still hard for me to completely trust anyone.

"Denise, would you go out on a date with me?" Ethan asked.

I was afraid to answer because I wanted to say yes but couldn't. "Ethan, I would like to, but I can't. I'm not ready. I'm so sorry." I knew he was hurt. I knew that nothing I said would help him feel better.

"Well, it's getting late and Carly still has to get everything set for tomorrow. Would you like a ride to school? We can sit together at the opening day assembly."

"That would be great. Thanks, Ethan. See you at seven tomorrow," I said as I walked toward my front door.

As I entered the house, the smell of spaghetti and garlic bread enveloped me. My mom was making our favorite dinner and the dinner she always made before my first day at school.

"Hey, Mom, dinner smells good," I said.

"Well, it's almost finished, so why don't you set the table?" she responded.

I just smiled, having already started setting the table.

We sat down to eat when my mom burst into tears. Same as she did the night before my freshman year of high school, claiming I was growing up too fast. I never knew what to say because when I tried to cheer her up, she smiled and started crying again.

Finally it was time to get some sleep before my senior year of high school. I was jumpy yet scared. I finally calmed down and fell asleep, realizing I wouldn't have to face the day alone because I would have Ethan. The best summer and soon school year would be all thanks to him. Being deep into my dreams, I realized this was the perfect ending to my perfect summer.

Chapter Seven

Senior

Climbing into Ethan's car, I was greeted with a smile. The drive to school was quiet yet energized. Finally, pulling into the parking lot, I knew I was able to officially call myself a senior. Ethan and I walked into auditorium, and I was amazed by how many students there were. It was hard to find a seat for the both of us, but we eventually did. The assembly was super boring—I actually saw some students fall asleep. Instead of going through all of the school rules that no one would follow, they should have just said, "Welcome to another year as CHS! Now come get your schedules. We have three lines, and it is all alphabetical. The end."

By the end of the torment of orientation, I went to get my schedule. This was where Ethan and I had to split. His last name was Graf while mine was Willow. When I got my schedule, I looked for Ethan right away, hoping we might have classes together. Unfortunately, when we found each other, we only had math together. He was in AP history class and regular English while I was in AP English and regular history—both excelling in the classes we hoped to one day major in.

I headed off to my writing class alone—one class I was looking forward to because I loved to write. It gave me an English credit as well without having to sit in a boring class. Mr. Star was my teacher, and he seemed to be very nice. The first assignment he gave us was to write a short story about an event in our life. If only I had an event I was willing to share.

I met up with Ethan at lunch. He couldn't stop talking about his history class. He was so excited about all of the past historical things he was going to learn. I didn't want to ruin his mood by reminding him that I hated history, so I just smiled and said, "That's great." We both had bought lunch, which for school food was surprisingly good. Too soon, though, we had to go our separate ways again. We made plans to meet at his car after class.

History was an okay class. My teacher wrote that his name was Mr. A. He wouldn't tell us what it stood for, though, just that he wanted to be called Mr. A. I could tell right away that he was very passionate about teaching history. He gave us our syllabus and told us that those who did not enjoy history would love our own pasts by the end of the year. I was not into history, but I knew our past as a nation helped create who we were today. Overall he seemed like a nice teacher, and I was happy that I seemed to be getting really great teachers.

The day flew by, and soon I was standing at Ethan's car, waiting on him. When I looked up, I saw him talking to a group of both guys and girls. I figured those were his friends from last year and decided to move to the door of the car instead of standing by the trunk. After about fifteen minutes of waiting, Ethan showed up to the car and was startled to see me.

"Denise, I'm so sorry. I was looking for you, but I didn't see you by the car. I would have introduced you to some of my friends. They were hoping to meet you, too. Maybe tomorrow," Ethan excitedly said.

"Sure, no problem. That sounds great," I said while climbing into the car. "Hey, Ethan, would you and Carly like to go out for Chinese with my mom and me? We go out for dinner after the first day of school, and it would be nice if you join us. Your dad can come, too, if you want him to." I didn't know why I wanted to invite Ethan, but it felt right to ask him to dinner. I was praying he would say yes, and I thought maybe I would like to hear all about Carly's first day.

"Sure, I'll see if Carly and I can go. My dad isn't really the public type unless he's going to play pool."

"We can swing by and pick up Carly before we head to my house, if you want."

"Well, maybe you should inform your mom first. Just give me a call to confirm us all going to dinner. I'll even drive, since I do know where the greatest Chinese restaurant is."

I couldn't help but smile and climb out of the car, seeing as we had arrived at my house. I promised to call him right after I talked to my mom and headed toward my front door. I watched his car head down the street before heading in the house.

As soon as I entered the door, I ran up to my room and threw my book bag in the chair next to my desk. I put my iPod in the dock and played some upbeat country music. I then proceeded to leave my room open and head to the bathroom and look in the mirror. I quickly washed my face and started to apply my makeup. I also started to have another flashback from when we first started these dinners.

"Mommy, Mommy, can I wear makeup, too?" I asked.

"Sure, why not? We can do this every year. How about that? Every year after the first day of school, we will get all fancy and wear makeup. We will dress like we are going to a fancy restaurant, too. How does that all sound?" She smiled.

"That sounds amazing, Mommy! I love you!"

I remembered how she smiled that day. I saw that smile on my lips when I looked back at myself in the mirror today.

I was just finishing putting my lip gloss on when I heard the front door open. I ran down the stairs and gave my mom a big hug.

"So Mom, are you ready for tonight?" I asked.

"What's tonight, dear?" she responded while looking at me wearing makeup.

"It's the dinner we do after the first day of school every year, Mom. How could you forget that? I also invited Ethan and Carly. Should I tell them to dress up as well?"

"Oh, Denise, sweetheart, I did forget. I'm so sorry and that is fine. Give them a call. I'll go get ready. Where are we going tonight?"

"We are going to a Chinese restaurant. Ethan said he would drive since he knows where the best Chinese restaurant is in town."

I followed her upstairs to finish getting dressed and call Ethan to let him know they were welcome to dinner.

Dinner was great. Everyone had fun. Carly went crazy telling us all about her first day at school and all of the kids she was making friends with. Ethan told everyone how his classes went and about how nice it was to meet up with his friends again. Then my mom looked to me, and I said I had really nice teachers. The rest of the night was filled with Carly's first day of school.

We were dropped off, and I headed upstairs after telling my mom goodnight. I walked in my room and did my homework. When I walked to my bathroom to get my shower, I stopped. Right there I knew, as I looked in the mirror. I saw a scared little girl. The one who hated being surrounded by people and needed the comfort of her mother. This girl was not ready for senior year.

Chapter Eight

Bad Boy

Waking up the next morning felt nice. I felt more confident about finding all of my classes again. I could not wait for math, the one class I had with Ethan. We had also made plans to go out for lunch. Ethan had beaten me to the car and was waiting for me.

Ethan smiled at me as I climbed in and asked, "Where to for lunch?"

"I don't know, you choose. I'm good with anything but Mexican food." I never liked Mexican food unless it was Taco Bell.

"How about we go for burgers?"

"Sounds good to me. Let's go."

The ride to the burger joint was quiet, and eating lunch was quiet as well. We headed back to school in silence that felt hours long. Finally, we made it to school and Ethan led us to math. We sat next to each other, by his friends he saw in the same class as us. The teacher was getting started with introductions, stating his name as Mr. Greene. When he told us the pages we needed to read in our books, the door of the classroom opened. Stepping through the door was the best-looking guy I had ever seen, aside from Ethan. His hair was jet black and was just above his deep green eyes. His smile was devilish, yet so charming, and the way his shirt clung tight to his chest would make any girl want him. I could see he was trouble, so I looked back to the book to start reading the pages assigned.

"You're late, why?" asked Mr. Greene.

"Overslept. Sorry, though it might be happening other times, too. So sorry for those times, too," said the guy who came and sat next to me.

I looked up only to see why he didn't sit somewhere else. The whole classroom was full. I went to look back toward my book and caught him staring at me. I hate when people stare, but I try to ignore it.

"So, you must be Mr. Carter. I expect you to be on time to my class. Next time the door will not be open," said Mr. Greene, pointing to the board with our reading assignment to the Carter guy.

Class was distracting. I didn't feel comfortable. All I could think was thank God we didn't have to sit in the same seats.

Ethan got up when the bell rang and waited for me to get my books together. The guy stood up and went to help me with my bag.

"Don't, please. I've got it," I said, pulling my book out of his hands.

"My name is James. Yours?" he asked.

"Denise. I've got to go," I said and turned to Ethan. "Ready to go?"

"Yep. I'll walk you to your next class," he said.

"Ethan, you don't have to, really. Your class is across campus from mine."

"Where are you headed?" asked James.

"I'm headed to 'History of the Arts' with Mrs. Wells." I sighed.

"Me too. I'll walk her there," he said to Ethan. "Don't worry; she will make it to class on time." He smirked.

Ethan didn't look very happy, but if he walked me to class he would be late, so I told him to go on. I'd meet him at the car after class. We parted, and I started walking toward my class with James walking beside me. I didn't talk to him or even want to talk to him, but he wanted to talk to me.

"So, is that guy your boyfriend or something?"

I didn't respond, just kept walking and went through the door to class and sat down. Of course, to my dismay, he sat next to me. Classes started and I was finally calming my nerves from having him staring at me when he passed me a piece of paper. I didn't even look at it, just handed it back. Instead of giving up, though, he handed it to me again. I didn't feel like playing, so I read the note.

If you ever need a ride anywhere, I can pick you up.

I scribbled back that I wouldn't need a ride.

Class ended shortly after, and I went to head out to meet Ethan at his car when I felt someone put their hand on my arm. It was James, who smiled at me and wouldn't let me go.

"Please, let me go," I said.

"Wait, I want to ask you something. Want to go out with me?" He smiled. His smile was gorgeous, but all I felt was his mysterious bad boy.

"No," was all I had to say. Then I pulled my arm and walked away.

He followed me to the car. "Why not? Is that guy your boyfriend?"

"He isn't. I said no. Are you hard of hearing?"

"You'll want to go out with me eventually. Every girl does. You're just playing hard to get."

About then was when Ethan showed up, and he didn't look very happy. "Why are you at my car?" he asked.

"Just talking to my new friend, Denise," James responded.

I heard the car door unlock, so I climbed in, not wanting to talk, just to get home. I saw Ethan look at James, then climb in the car. He took me home in silence, and I could see he was mad but I didn't understand why.

"Ethan, why are you so upset?" I had to ask.

"I'm not upset, I'm jealous. I don't like the way James looks at you, and I've known him for years. He gets any girl he wants, and then when he has gotten all of her, he throws her away like she is trash. I've only seen one girl turn away from him, and eventually he got her as well."

It was weird to think that Ethan was jealous over someone I barely knew. I told him not to worry. I would give him a chance before I gave James the chance to try and destroy me. He didn't look like my words would make a difference. He looked scared, as if he was going to lose me.

I climbed out of the car and told him I'd see him tomorrow. I headed toward my front door as I heard his car pull out of the driveway.

A few minutes later, my mom was walking through the door with dinner and coffee. I smiled and told her she was my hero for the coffee. All I wanted to do was forget the day had happened, but I had about two hours of homework to do. I kissed my mom on the cheek before heading upstairs to get started on my homework.

I decided to join an after-school writing class, which happened to start tonight. Before the teacher arrived, I started doodling on my paper. I heard someone sit down next to me, and when I looked up the last person on earth I wanted to see was sitting there. James flashed his charming smile at me. I could not wait for this class to be over, and I was not planning on coming back. This was my first and last class with this group.

When class did end, James watched me. I felt him and I wanted to yell, "Take a picture!" but I didn't. I calmly turned to him and asked, "What are you staring at?"

"Well, I'm staring at what I want and wondering what you would do if I went to kiss you," he said while moving closer to me.

"Well, you can't have what you're staring at, and you're not my type, sorry."

I didn't mean that, though, because every guy was not my type. I couldn't trust, so how could I have a type? I walked away and slowly processed everything that had happened.

On the drive home, I thought of Ethan and James, the differences and similarities between them. The way they both acted around me and how one was kind while the other was straight forward. I was still thinking of this all as I walked through the door and went up the stairs to bed.

I crawled into my bed, lying with my eyes open in the darkness. I didn't know how to turn my mind off from going through the day. One part stood out the most that played over and over again. The class I had with Ethan and the way he looked at James when James started talking to me. It was as if a battle had begun: good guy verses bad boy. In the end, all I could think through before finally falling asleep was hoping my heart wouldn't let in someone who could destroy it. If I ever fell for James, he could destroy me just like the type of boy he was—a bad boy.

Chapter Nine

Confused

Waking up early wasn't fun at all. I definitely was not looking forward to school, not after the stress of yesterday. When Ethan picked me up, I was not in the greatest mood. Neither was he, though, so the tension in the car was overwhelming. When we finally pulled into the parking lot, I had to break the silence and tension in the air.

"Ethan, are you mad at me?" I felt as if I had done something wrong. When I looked up at him and saw the look on his face, I realized that was the wrong question to ask.

"Of course I'm not mad at you, Denise. How could you think that?" he responded sadly.

"Well, you just look really mad, and you've barely talked to me since James did. I just thought I did something wrong."

"Denise, I could never be mad at you. I'm frustrated at the fact that James decides he wants you and won't leave you alone. I don't want to see him hurt you. I've seen what he can do to a girl."

He looked so upset, and I didn't know how to take his pain away. I grabbed my bag and climbed out of the car, going to his side and meeting him. He looked at me with a confused look, and then I gave him a hug. We had never hugged because I didn't trust myself with my feelings, but my friend needed a hug, so I gave it to him. I could tell I had shocked him by the way he tensed, then relaxed and hugged me back tightly.

"Aw, so he is your boyfriend," smirked a person I wished wasn't really there.

When I released Ethan and turned around, a smirking James looked at me. I felt Ethan tense again and knew he was still angry with James.

"He's my friend, unlike you. So if you could just leave us alone and go show up to whatever class you want to be late to today, that would be great," I responded.

It felt weird to be standing up for myself against him, against someone whose eyes pierced right through me and made me feel like he could see my soul. I pulled Ethan with me so that he wouldn't start a fight with James. I just wanted Ethan to be happy. Before class, we met up with his friends and he introduced me to them. They all seemed nice and welcomed me into their group. I still felt like an outsider, but I didn't want to tell Ethan that. He was happy that I was meeting his friends.

Before I headed to class, Ethan asked me if I wanted to meet him outside for lunch to sit in the front lawn. Thinking of how nice the sun felt, I smiled and agreed to meet him. I gave him another hug, then turn to walk toward my English class.

Walking into class, I sat down in the second row and pulled out our homework assignment. I didn't notice someone sitting by me until I was asked what I had lying on my desk. I really hoped I was dreaming, but when I looked to my left I saw that charming smile that seemed to be showing up everywhere.

James looked at me, and I glared back. I didn't understand how he could be in three of my classes, including one he hadn't even been in on Monday.

"What are you doing in this class? You weren't here Monday or Tuesday, so why are you here right now?" I asked.

"Well, you see, the class I was supposed to be in was the wrong grade level, so I was put in here instead. I thought I would dread having English this early, but I can see I was right to show up on time," he smirked.

I didn't want to believe he was in my class, so I got my stuff and moved to a seat that was in the middle of a crowd of people. I knew if I was going to do well in this class, I couldn't be sitting next to James. He looked back at me but then turned around when the teacher walked into the classroom.

Class was the same as Monday. We talked about the essays we had been assigned and learned how to correct them and what to look for in an essay.

Overall, the class went smoothly, and soon I would be away from James and with the only person I felt comfortable with at this school: Ethan.

As I was on my way to meet Ethan for lunch, I started thinking about everything that had me going against my own trust, the feelings that had developed for Ethan that I chose to ignore, the way James looked at me and got my heart thumping. I knew James was bad and would hurt me, yet I was attracted to him. Ethan, though, was so sweet and kind, and I didn't know if he would hurt me or not, but I cared for him. This was all running through my head on the walk to the bench, where I saw Ethan.

"Hey, you. How was English class?" He smiled.

"It was great. Except for the new member who joined the class today; James got moved to my English class, but after he sat by me, I moved. How long do you think it will take him to give up on me?"

"Denise, I've never seen him give up on a girl. That's probably because I've never seen a girl turn him down. He usually gets what he wants and no one asks questions. That's what he did in middle school, and he has already gone out with two girls like that this year, and we are only in our third day of school. He dumped each after one day, said they were missing something."

"Wow, so in other words, he's going to keep bugging me."

"Unless you have a boyfriend, James doesn't mess with other guys' girls. He just waits for the relationship to end."

"I could always fake a boyfriend, and then I wouldn't have him staring at me all class."

"Won't work. I've seen girls try."

I took a bite of my sandwich as I thought of ways to try and get the bad news out of this new life of mine. Overall, my lunch with Ethan was just like those summer days we spent together. All that was missing was his little sister. Everything that was on my mind went away as I sat there with Ethan, until we had to leave. We agreed to meet by his car at the end of the day.

My next class I attended was back to being with people I didn't know. It flew by and too soon I was walking to Ethan's car by myself. With my books in hand and walking lost in my thoughts, all I could do was believe that until I could learn to trust my feelings, I would remain confused.

Chapter Ten

I'll Try

After spending the day dealing with James and hanging with Ethan and his friends, I was ready for the weekend. Overall, I only had one class to myself, and the rest were with James. I only had one with Ethan. The weekend I had to myself while my mother was at work when I woke up Saturday morning. I had two papers to write and tons of math homework to do. My first week at school had gone by faster than I could blink an eye and was full of enough events to last me a year.

I was feeling very lazy, so I slowly descended the stairs and sat on the couch in some sweats. Sitting on the couch, I looked around to really see the house I had been living in for almost four months. The walls were my mother's favorite shade of lavender. She had painted the house herself, and I wasn't there to help. I felt as if I had been a bad daughter, like I didn't help her with anything that was connected to this house. I looked into the kitchen and saw that my mother hadn't painted the walls yet. I then proceeded to go up to her room and see that she hadn't painted those walls, either. Looking around, I realized how I could help my mom today.

Running to my room, I hurried and changed. Grabbing my purse and keys off the hook, I ran to the used car my mother had bought me yesterday for school. Driving around, I finally found a store with paint and got forget-me-not blue, sunflower yellow, and the prettiest purple I could find, light lavender that matched the dress I wore for my mother's wedding. It was her favorite color. Along with those paints, I grabbed some stencils and black paint to decorate.

When I arrived home, I moved all the furniture to the family room from the kitchen. Running upstairs, I grabbed an old shirt and sweats and quickly pulled my hair back into a messy bun so I could be ready to paint. As I headed down the stairs, I heard my phone go off and quickly read over the text. It was from my mom, letting me know she would be home late, which was helpful since that would mean I'd have more time to paint. I smiled, then headed downstairs to the stereo in the family room and turned on my favorite radio station. While dancing to the beat of each song and painting, I ended up having loads of fun being home alone.

When the kitchen was finally finished, I grabbed the purple and went to my mother's room. Looking around, I realized this room wouldn't be as easy to paint. I looked at the furniture and thought about calling Ethan to help me move it, but then I went against that thought. I was determined to do this myself for my mother and to have a boy-less, stress-free weekend. With that in mind, I scooted the furniture into the middle of the room the best I could and covered it with plastic, along with the floor.

When I finally finished her room, I headed to mine. Moving the furniture and covering it with plastic, I painted my room as well. When I finished the base coats of the painting and looked at the clock, I was shocked. It had only taken me three hours to paint all three rooms. I figured it would only take me another hour to do the stencil work, so I went to sit on the couch to take a breather. When I looked up, I saw someone at my window. When I went to the window, though, all I saw were the little boys across the street visiting their grandmother.

I figured this was a sign that I should finish what I started so I could move the furniture back in time. As if seeing someone at the window could mean I might not finish before my mother would walk through the door. In the kitchen, I wrote over the doorway, "You Are My Sunshine," my mother's favorite thing to say when I was a little girl. Then in her room over her bed, I wrote: "Single Moms Make the World Go 'Round." I knew it was something that would cheer her up.

Taking the stencil to my room, I looked around and thought about what I wanted to put on my wall. Suddenly, I had to turn to the computer and look up my favorite line in a song. Looking up the lyrics to the song I used to listen to all the time, I found that part I was looking for. "With you by my side, I will fight and defend," the strongest lyrics I know, in the song "Keep Holding On." I carefully stenciled those words around my room as a border on the top and the bottom of my room. When I finally finished, I left so my room could dry.

Heading to my mom's room, I quickly pushed the furniture back to its original place. After I finished in my mom's room, I headed downstairs to the kitchen to put it all back then start on dinner.

For dinner I was cooking lasagna, my mother's favorite food. When she walked through the door, I was sitting on the couch watching television, waiting on dinner to be finished.

"Smells good. What did you make?" my mother asked while hanging her keys on the key hook.

"I made lasagna, your favorite!" I smiled.

"What is the occasion?"

"Nothing, but dinner is almost finished. I want to show you something after dinner, so just sit here until then and finish watching this show with me."

She smiled and sat down to finish watching the show. When the show was over, I got up and served dinner. We both sat down and had a lovely dinner, and my mother looked around the kitchen.

"So is this what you did today? You painted the kitchen?"

"That's not all I did. Look above the door." I smiled.

"Denise, it's wonderful."

"Well, that's not all I did. Finish your dinner so I can show you the rest."

We finished the dinner, and I showed her my room, where she helped me move my furniture back. She really liked the way I painted it as well and was shocked when I said I did more. Closing her eyes and pulling her to her room, I had her open her eyes. She looked around, then read the saying over her bed. When I looked at her, I saw tears in her eyes.

"Mom, are you okay?!" I was worried I had upset her.

"Denise, I can't believe you did all this today. It's beautiful."

"Well, what else could I do for a mom as great as you?"

"Denise, I'm sorry. I messed up," she said while pulling me to sit on the bed with her. She looked in my eyes and continued. "I feel so bad for messing up with you. I feel like I've ruined your life. I'm sorry. I wasn't the best role model for you. You never had a dad really around and the whole lie that I should have found out. I am sorry. It's my fault you can't open your heart and trust. It's my fault that you might be missing out on being with someone who could be your soul mate. Ethan really likes you, Denise, and he deserves a chance. I don't want you to miss out because of me, Denise. I want you to have what I never did."

"Mom, I didn't know that is how you felt. You didn't mess up, Mom. You did everything right. I wouldn't be the strong, independent woman I am today without you. I know I have trust issues with people and that it's hard for me to open up, but I'm going to think about giving Ethan a chance. I feel like he might not hurt me. I promise, Mom, I'm working over my fears. I don't want to be afraid anymore."

I gave my mom the biggest hug and said, "I'll try."

Chapter Eleven

FAITH

The weekend flew by, and my mom and I spent all of Sunday together. Ethan picked me up Monday morning, and the conversation between my mother and I flew into my head. When Ethan saw me, I was all smiles for him. When he looked at me, I saw his smile and knew that overcoming my fear with him might heal all of the scars I had from my past.

"Why are you all smiles today? Got a hot date or something?" He laughed.

"Nope. I just had a refreshing weekend and thought about a lot of stuff, but that will have to wait until lunch. Well, since we've been eating in the garden and it's so pretty, I've decided I want to tell you something there." I smiled.

He looked at me strangely but took what I had said. Walking me to class, I knew I was ready to work over my fears. For the first time in a long time, I felt like I wasn't afraid to head forward into my life. I wasn't afraid to see how my life might turn out. All I could see for the first time ever was that just maybe I wouldn't have to go through everything on my own.

James kept attempting to talk to me, but I wasn't going to let him damper my mood. All I could think was that I couldn't wait for this class to end.

"Hey, girly, what was up with you today? Are you finally falling in love with me? Ready to go out?" James smirked.

"No, I'm not going to go out with you. I'm in a good mood, and I'm not letting you ruin my good mood," I replied.

"What, did that loser Ethan finally ask you to go out with him?"

"No, he did not, and why do you care?"

"I don't care, really, just think that you deserve me, but for some reason you don't want to give me a chance," he said while going to stroke my cheek. "So the only question I can think is, what is it about him that you like?"

"Well, let's see, he doesn't stroke my cheek. He doesn't act like it would be an honor to know him, let alone be approached by him, and he isn't a complete ass."

"That is harsh, Denise. I just want go out with you, that's all."

I turned around and left him to go meet up with Ethan.

"Hey, Ethan, sorry I was running late. James held me up," I apologized.

"What did he want? Probably asking you out again, wasn't he? Do you want me to tell him to back off, that you don't want a boyfriend?" he rambled with an angry expression.

"Ethan, that's what I was going to talk to you about, actually. See, my mom and I were talking two nights ago about my fear and how to overcome it. Well, I've decided that I'm ready to—"

"ETHAN!"

We both turned to see who had yelled his name. When I saw where that voice came from, I felt my body crumble. She was beautiful and blonde, almost goddess like. She walked over to us so perfectly and hugged Ethan, pressing closely to him even after the hug.

"Faith? What are you doing here? I thought you moved years ago," Ethan responded.

"Well, I did, silly, but I'm back for senior year. I figured you would be here still and single, so I thought we could pick up where we left off. We were the power couple in middle school until I moved away eighth-grade year. Plus, it's not like you have a girlfriend or anything," Faith said while glancing over at me.

"I haven't heard from you since you moved away, Faith. We both have changed. You might find you don't like me anymore, and I've moved on."

"Do you have a girlfriend right now?"

"Well, no, but—"

"Well, see, so you will pick me up at seven tonight, right? Oh, wait, you don't know my new address. You're still living at the same place, right? Of course you are. I'll see you at seven. We can catch up and go on a date." Faith smiled, then kissed him on the cheek and walked away.

I didn't know what to say considering the conversation I was going to have with him would have been pointless now. His ex-girlfriend was back, and they would soon be back together. She was beautiful, so why would he ever want to look at me as more than a friend? I snuck away when she kissed him on the cheek and ate my lunch alone. My hope was gone. Taken away by Faith.

Chapter Twelve

Hidden

Later that day, on the way home with Ethan, the car was silent. I was upset, but I tried to act normal. Ethan knew something was up, but I couldn't tell him it was because I wanted to be with him. I made him wait, and I realized that by having him wait, I didn't deserve him at all.

"Denise, you are very quiet. Are you okay?"

"Yeah," I replied. "I'm just a little tired, wasn't feeling too well after lunch. I think I might have a bug. Someone in my first period was coughing a lot, so I might be sick. Nothing to worry about." I forced a smile.

"So, what did you want to tell me at lunch? When Faith left, you were gone. I even looked around, but you completely disappeared." He paused and soon continued shortly after before I could speak. "Faith was my girlfriend in high school, and we broke up before she left. She cheated on me with James, but she thought we broke up because I figured out she was moving. She doesn't know that I found out about her and James."

"Oh, I'm so sorry about that. Did you get a chance to talk to her about that, or are you going to tell her tonight on your date?"

"I'm not going on the date with her. I actually wanted to ask you about that. Will you come to my house and pretend to be my girlfriend, just to get her to leave me alone? I know we are just friends, but like James, she won't back off unless I'm taken."

"Well, uh, I guess I could, since we are friends, but she will see you at school, and she will know you are not really going out with me. Plus,

I don't want to ruin your reputation when you are known to date girls that beautiful."

I didn't know why I said all of those things. I couldn't understand why I didn't tell him what I wanted to tell him about me wanting to be his girlfriend. That I wanted to try and do something unplanned in my life and not know what my future held.

He dropped me off and let me know he would text me when he arrived home. I thanked him for the ride and walked into the house and up to my room, turning my phone volume up as I walked up the stairs.

My mind was jumbled and I was upset. I didn't want just be his friends. I wanted to move forward with my life and be surprised again. I wanted to overcome my fear of being with someone, but I didn't want to be with just anyone. I wanted to be with Ethan. My mom would tell me to explain this to Ethan, but I was still afraid of rejection. Faith was beautiful, while I was so plain. I wore makeup, but I'd never look as goddess like as she did.

While I was sitting on my bed, thinking about all of this, my phone went off, but instead of a text, it was ringing. I looked at the caller ID and didn't recognize the number, so I let it go to voicemail. About ten minutes later, I received another call, but it was from Ethan.

"Hey, Denise, you never told me what you wanted to ask me at lunch or tell me. It seemed really important and looked like it was something that put the smile on your face this morning just thinking about it. So what did you want to tell me?" he asked.

"Ethan, it is not really important anymore. I just wanted to tell you about my fears, I guess. No big deal…." I felt so depressed saying that.

"Wait, you think you may have found a way to get over your fears and you say it is not a big deal?!"

"Well, yes, because it's pointless now. I waited too long for me to even try what I had as an idea."

"Well, maybe it's not too late. Tell me what the plan was."

"Maybe another day, after your speak with Faith. You said she might have changed and that you might have changed. You might find out you want to go back out with her, and I don't want you to be thinking of me when you are speaking to her."

"I told you, Denise, I'm not going to go back out with Faith. I have feelings for someone else, and I don't see those feelings going away anytime soon."

"Who do you have feelings for?"

"Well, she is a beautiful girl who is shy, kind, loving, and funny, and she is also very guarded. She looks amazing in shorts and tank tops as well."

"Are you talking about my mom? That is gross, Ethan!" I couldn't help but laugh after I said that.

"No, more like your mom's daughter. Denise, I care about you, and if I was going to ask anyone or go anywhere with anyone, I would want that someone to be you."

"You really mean that, don't you?"

"Yes, and if you think you found a way to get over your fear, I'm assuming you have developed feelings for someone. I'm hoping that someone is me."

I paused, not knowing what to say. I knew right then and there I could tell him that, yes, it was him. I wanted to be his girlfriend, and I wanted him to be my boyfriend. I took a deep breath and said exactly that.

"Ethan, you're right. I have developed feelings for someone, and that someone is you. I thought I was ready, then I saw Faith by you and I crumbled so easily. I don't know if—"

"Denise, stop! Don't say anything to cause doubt. Just say that you will be my girlfriend and forget about Faith. She means nothing to me. Be here for me when she comes over, and I'll show you that she means nothing. You're the only girl I see."

I smiled and spoke once more before hanging up and heading down to see my mom. "Ethan, if you want me to be there, meet me halfway. I'll start walking. Also, I would love to be your girlfriend."

Running down the stairs to fill my mom in, I was thinking one thing. One thing that kept making my smile grow until it was so big, and my mom just knew what I was going to tell her. That thought was that for the first time in a long time, I would not have to keep my feelings hidden.

Chapter Thirteen

Coming True

Spending the night with Ethan had been a dream. We sat on his couch and cuddled while watching movies. Being in his arms felt right, just the way I thought it would. Even when Faith showed up and I saw her glare at me, I was in a good mood because I was with Ethan. I ended up falling asleep in his arms, and he called my mom, letting her know I was safe and asking if I could sleep there since I was already on the couch. Trusting him and me, she agreed, and I fell deeper asleep, snuggled up with Ethan.

Waking up the next morning, I found myself wrapped in a blanket and on a couch. Thinking that I should be aching by now, I sat up and realized the reason I was so comfortable. Ethan had stayed with me all night. He had been my pillow all night, and he slept sitting up. I felt so bad for him but so happy that he had stayed with me at the same time. Realizing that we seemed to be moving slightly fast, I realized all the time spent in the summer had made this time we spent feel perfect instead of too fast. I didn't want to admit to myself, but I could barely hold it in as I looked over at his sleeping face. I had fallen in love with Ethan, and I hadn't even known it. I would never admit this to him—not even wild horses could pull that information out of me right now. All I knew was I loved Ethan, and for the first time, not only was I not scared, but I felt whole again. As if I had never had those scars from my past, it was as if I was right where I belonged.

"Hey, sleepyhead," I heard him say as his eyes fluttered open and looked down on me.

"Morning. Did I wake you?" I smiled.

"Nope. Just woke up on my own. Must be the way I fell asleep. I meant to let you sleep in my room while I slept out here, but we both must have fallen asleep."

"It's okay. I don't mind that you fell asleep out here with me. It's nice waking up to you."

I couldn't help but smile as I saw him blush at my words. He looked so cute with those blue eyes that I fell in love with. I realized he was mine and I was his. I felt that everything was right. I didn't want to get up and go, but I knew I had to go home so I could get ready for school.

Sitting up, I stretched and stood, looking back at Ethan. He looked up at me and knew I was getting ready to head home. Following me to the door seemed just like it had during the summer. When I turned to say goodbye and "See you in a few hours," I was surprised with a kiss.

Ethan had kissed me. He was the second guy to ever kiss me. The kiss ended too soon and felt so magical. His lips, so soft against mine, seemed to fit. I was lost for words as I headed out the door. Heading home, my smile was huge and my lips burned from the way Ethan's lips had felt against mine.

Time flew by, and I was soon sitting in class next to Ethan, listening to our teacher and doodling on my paper while looking at Ethan every once in a while. I was also having fun ignoring James. He seemed as if he was in the background rather than a pest who needed to be front and center. Ethan and I ate lunch in the courtyard again and cuddled while we worked on plans for his little sister's birthday. With his arm around me while I wrote in my notebook, getting kisses on my forehead, cheek, and neck felt like a fantasy. Every place he kissed burned after his lips left that spot. It was a good burn but still a burn. I wondered if this meant I would never have to be afraid ever again. If he was the person everyone said would be my Prince Charming. If I was really living a fairytale or was just a lucky girl.

We soon had to part for our last classes but would meet back at his car. He walked me to class and gave me a light kiss that lit up my smile.

The next thing I knew, my class was over, and I was walking to his car. Before I got to him, though, I ran into someone and dropped all of my books.

Looking up, getting ready to apologize, I stopped myself. Standing in front of me with a look of pure hatred was Faith.

"You think you are so special because you're with Ethan, don't you? Saw that he was going to go back out with me and had to snatch him up. Afraid you were going to lose your best friend? Well, I have news for you. You're nothing compared to me. He is just with you to make me jealous. I'm the only one he loves, and you are just a toy to him. As soon as he sees that he misses me, he will drop you like that. You better learn your place here, new girl, because I know you're new to this town. He is mine," she practically growled.

I didn't say anything but got my stuff and headed for Ethan's car. So much for living the fairytale. Faith was who brought me back to reality. She was the crack to my dreams coming true.

Chapter Fourteen

Grace

When I arrived at Ethan's car, I couldn't help but smile when I saw him. He, of course, knew something was wrong before I could even say a word.

"What's wrong? Did something happen? Is James still bugging you?" Ethan asked.

"No, he is not bugging me. I just ran into Faith, that's all. She isn't happy we are dating. She believes you are using me to make her jealous," I mumbled.

He pulled me into a hug and then whispered into my ear, "I would never use you. If I wanted to make someone jealous, it would be to get you to go out with me, not her. I have the person I want to be with right here with me."

I smiled and lightly kissed his chest. Even though it had only been a day of dating, it felt as if we had been together for months. So when we got to my house, it felt natural to be holding his hand while he drove. It felt natural to walk hand in hand inside my house and sit on my couch, cuddled while doing homework. Everything about us felt so natural. What else I could ask for in the world? I had no idea and didn't expect to know until it was thrown at me.

"Want something to drink? Mom wants you to stay for dinner. She figures that we are dating, but she sent me a text asking if you would stay," I said.

"Of course, I would love to stay for dinner. Your mom's and your cooking is the best. If I could, I would come over every night for dinner. That and to see you." He smiled.

"Well, you are in luck, my friend, because you are invited over every night!" I laughed.

Everything about being with Ethan was easy after that night. He stayed for dinner, watched a movie before leaving, and gave me a kiss. It was perfect, at least while I was awake.

When I went to sleep, I had nightmares where Faith was forcing me to watch her and Ethan make out. She proved that she was right by getting Ethan to cheat on me. She was the star of these nightmares, and I was always suffering, whether being tied up and tortured to watch them or discovering it on my own with her friends' help. It continued for weeks.

After four months of school and three and a half months of dating Ethan, I realized I needed someone else in my life. I didn't realize it until Ethan and I hung out with his friends and it seemed like all we did was either be with each other alone or with his friends. Never mine. I realized this would be because I didn't really have any friends and that would be because I couldn't open up to people. Ethan had been my friend, but now he was my boyfriend. I decided the next level to overcoming my fear was to get a friend and to have someone else I could trust.

Ironically, while I was sitting in my English writing class, a girl I had never seen sat next to me. I didn't know if that was a sign, but I took it as one.

"Hi, my name is Denise. Yours?" I asked her.

"My name is Grace. I like your bracelet," she said.

"Thanks. My boyfriend gave it to me for helping out with his sister's birthday party. Do you have anyone you sit with at lunch? I mean, would you like to sit with us at lunch, if you don't already have plans?" I hoped she would say yes.

"Sure, are you heading there after class?"

"I am. We can walk together. I think this might be a beginning to a great friendship."

"I do, too. Thanks for inviting me."

It was a longshot that she would be nice to me, and I was happy I took that risk and talked to her. Maybe her and my friendship would grow as fast as my relationship with Ethan. Maybe for the first time ever, I would have a best friend. I got a good vibe from this girl. I could see my life changing with not only Ethan but my new friend, Grace.

Chapter Fifteen

Fun

At lunch I introduced Ethan and Grace. Ethan smiled up at me, knowing I was working toward opening up more. Grace seemed to be nice and ended up talking to me about the same books and why we both chose the path we did. All together we made a really nice group.

About ten minutes till the end of lunch, one of Ethan's friends, Ryan, showed up.

"Hey, Denise. Hey, Ethan, dude, I need to borrow your book for next period," Ryan said.

"Hey, Ryan, this is Grace, my friend," I spoke before Ethan could say anything.

"Dude, why don't you just go buy a new book if you need one?" responded Ethan.

"Hello, Grace, and Ethan, I will when I have the money. Until then I can't go buy a new book," Ryan said.

Ethan looked at me, rolled his eyes, then handed his book over to Ryan. Ryan thanked Ethan, then ran to class.

"You are such a nice guy, Ethan." I giggled.

"I try but if I wasn't nice to Ryan, he would be lost in school. He is the same as he was all through high school. Some people never change." Ethan sighed.

"You knew Ryan in high school?" Grace asked.

"Yep, he and I are best friends."

Grace was looking at me as if she needed my help. I knew her silence the whole time Ryan was with us meant she had developed feelings for Ryan.

Either that or she had feelings for him all through high school and just realized that maybe since she knew his friends, she could get to know him.

"Grace, tonight being Friday and everything, would you like to come over and spend the night? Ethan takes me home and he stays for dinner. Would you like to join us?" I wanted to get to know Grace and really be friends with her.

"Sounds like fun, if Ethan doesn't mind me intruding on dinner with you two…." She trailed off.

"Any friend of my sweetheart is a friend of mine. Plus it will be nice to have someone else at the table." He smiled.

Grace smiled, then headed to class while Ethan walked me to mine. Before heading into class, I turned and looked up at him. He looked different, more serious than usual. I took my hand up and placed it on his cheek. He leaned into my hand, and I knew something was wrong.

"We will talk on the way home," was all he said before kissing me with such strength that it didn't feel like one of his kisses.

I walked into class, worried.

Class flew by, and I walked over to his car. Waiting by the car, I looked for Ethan, still unable to not worry. When I saw Ethan, he looked like he was distracted by something. I didn't like that he was worried. I wanted to help him, but I didn't know what was wrong or how to help.

"Hey, sweetheart, are you okay?" he said when he saw the worried look on my face.

"Well, I'm worried about you. Since you dropped me off at class, you seem so distracted, and that kiss was not one of your kisses. It was like a goodbye kiss. I haven't experienced one, but I've heard or read about them," I said.

"Oh, I'm so sorry, Denise. I got a text that worried me and had me thinking about a lot of stuff. Faith still had my number and texted me, letting me know her little sister was going to the same school as Carly. She hoped that Carly would be okay at school. I have this feeling Faith is going to have her sister do something. I wouldn't put it past Faith, and until I know what, I don't know what to do. On top of all that, she said if I want it to end I would have to leave you, which I can't do, but I don't want Carly to get hurt."

"Ethan, I don't want Carly to get hurt. If we have to be friends only, then I mean it will be for the good cause. I love Carly and I don't want her hurt."

It hurt me to say that. I didn't only love Carly, but I loved Ethan as well. I didn't want to be apart from him, but I didn't want to make him choose, either.

"Grace is sleeping over, so why don't you spend time with Carly tonight instead of coming over? You need to do what you need to do to keep your family safe."

"Denise, look at me." He placed his hand under my chin to have me look at him. "I will never leave you. We will just have to figure something out. I'm not going to let Faith win—promise. I'm sorry I worried you. I...."

He kissed me and it felt normal again. It sounded as if he was going to say he loved me, but he didn't.

Dropping me off at home, I got ready for dinner and warned my mom about Grace spending the night. Dinner flew by, and soon it was time for Ethan to head home.

"I'll call you tomorrow, sweetheart." He smiled, kissed me, then headed out.

"So you two must have need dating for a long time. I mean, you guys look very close," Grace said.

"We've been together for three months, actually, but it seems like we have liked each way longer. I've liked him and him me, but I had this issue that made it impossible to date. Lot to learn about each other, but let's have some fun." I smiled.

"Sounds good to me. So what is on the agenda of fun?"

"Scary movies, talking to get to know each other better, and I have this really cool computer game I can show you."

"Sounds good. So what does your room look like?"

"Oh, follow me. I'm so sorry."

We ran up the stairs and stayed in my room the rest of the time. We laughed and squealed at how similar we were. It was the most fun I had in the longest time, aside from being with Ethan. Grace was the greatest and easiest friend I could be with. Overall, fixing everything and spending the night with Grace could be explained in one word. It was fun!

Chapter Sixteen

Keeping Together

The next morning, Grace and I were woken up by my phone. Ethan was calling us, and I scrambled off the bed, searching for where my phone had fallen. Quickly apologizing to Grace for the phone, I answered it.

"Morning," I mumbled, still not completely awake for a normal conversation.

"Morning, baby. How was the sleepover? Did I wake you two up?" he asked.

"Yeah, you woke us up, but it's okay. We needed to get up anyway, and the sleepover was fun. Grace and I have a lot in common. We actually were going to go to the bookstore today to find this book that came out this week."

"Mind if Carly and I join you? Carly really wants to see you, and I do, too."

"How sweet. Grace just said she doesn't mind, so pick us up in twenty?"

"Sounds like a plan."

We hung up, and then Grace and I hurried to get ready for when Ethan arrived. I was excited to have my friend, my boyfriend, and the cutest little girl to be in my life. Nothing seemed like it could go wrong. I had forgotten about Faith until I saw her vehicle sitting outside. Running out with Grace behind me, I was not afraid of her. I knew I would have to stand up to her.

"Morning, girls. Did you two sleep okay? I'm surprised to see you so bright today, Denise. I figured Ethan would have broken up with you to protect Carly," she sneered.

"You want Ethan and I to break up so you don't threaten his sister? He and I both love her, and she has nothing to do with our relationship. You come to me with your issue, you fight me," I practically growled.

"Oh, I know how you work. I know girls like you. Talk tough but secretly weak. I can take you down, no problem, and I will get Ethan back. I mean, one kiss, you there to watch, and victory is mine. I promise I will get him, and I figured you were going to say that. I would never hurt Carly. It was a threat because if I hurt Carly, Ethan would come after me and I don't want that if he is going to be my boyfriend."

"Faith, just shut up! He doesn't love you anymore, and he didn't break up with you because you were leaving town. He left because you slept with James. He knows that you cheated on him. Everyone knew and finally he found out!" Grace yelled.

"How the hell would you of all people know that?" Faith said.

She had such venom in her voice, I knew it was true. She had cheated on Ethan, and she had seriously thought she had gotten away with it. Before Grace or I could respond, though, Ethan's Explorer pulled in the driveway.

"What are you doing here, Faith?" he questioned.

"I was here to see if you broke up with her. But it seems that you don't care about your sister. Such a shame." She sighed.

"I know you would never hurt Carly. She isn't a part of it, and that was a threat. After thinking about it, I knew not to take your words seriously. I don't love you and you never loved me. I know about you and James, and I want you to get out of here. Never talk to Denise or Grace or me again. I'm in love with Denise, and nothing will separate us unless we want to be separated."

Hearing him say he loved me sent chills down my spine. Not knowing if he said it because he wanted to get Faith to leave him alone or because he meant it was torturing. All I knew was that if he meant it, I would let him know how I really felt. More importantly, I would get even more help to get Grace and Ryan together. For the first time in the presence of Faith, I couldn't help but smile up at Ethan.

Realizing what he had said, he smiled and looked at me. Knowing within that smile that he meant it, I couldn't help but kiss him right in front of everyone. We only separated when we heard a bloodcurdling scream. Faith had let out a scream full of so much hatred because she knew she would never win. We loved each other, and that was all that mattered.

Grace smiled at us, and we all watched as Faith's car pulled away. We had all stuck together, and I finally knew how Ethan felt and that he felt the same as me.

"Ethan, I love you, too." I smiled before kissing him again.

"I hate to interfere with this little yuck fest, but I think there is a little girl waiting on us." Grace laughed.

We all smiled and headed over to the car. Going to the bookstore, I realized we finally would be together with no distractions. Faith was gone, James had given up, and Ethan and I were happy. Grace just would need to be with Ryan, and I wanted to help her with that. More than anything, I realized that by sticking together we fought our fears of separation. It proved that nothing could be more important than keeping together.

Chapter Seventeen

Double Dating

The weekend had flown by. Ethan and I were unstoppable, and I was working through my fears. I had overcome my trust issues, and Ethan and Grace were proof of that. I fell in love with someone and opened up to him. I had made a friend and opened up to her. I stood up to the bully and had my friends behind me to back me up. My life felt more like my life than the way I was living before. I felt like I was actually living instead of planning everything out. My mother was so happy for me. She always had a smile these days—a real smile, not the fake one she has had since the divorce. More importantly, everyone who should be together were going to be together.

Ethan and I had set up a double date with my friend Grace and Ethan's friend Ryan. Both knew each other, and Ryan had a thing for Grace but didn't believe she liked him since she never talked to him. Grace was head over heels for Ryan but was too afraid to talk to him. We tried to get them to go out alone, but it didn't go so well, so we set up a double date.

"Denise, I don't know about this. I can barely talk to him at school. What makes you think having you and Ethan there will help me talk to Ryan?" Grace asked.

"Well, I'll be there to help relax you and fill in the blanks for when you lose your voice. Just remember, he does like you and he really wants to go out with you." I smiled.

"He said he likes me?" She gushed.

"How could he not? Grace, you're pretty, smart, and have a killer body. Curves in all the right places, not to mention you can look beautiful with or without makeup," I said.

She was so excited, and we were getting ready. To keep her mind off of all the loss of words she might have, we ended up talking about the new couple at school. James and Faith had finally decided to get together. They had been going out for almost two months and cheated on each other whenever they wanted. Nothing would break up that power couple. I was happy that Grace and I could laugh about Faith and James, and I was even happier that Grace would be happy after tonight.

The boys were getting ready and meeting us at the pizza shack down the road, so my mom let us borrow her car. Driving over there, I realized that Grace was getting ready to go into her panic mode, a mode I tried desperately to keep away.

"Grace, stop worrying. He will love you! I bet he has been crushing on you as long as you have had a thing for him. Just relax and talk to him. Tonight is your night!" I grinned.

"You're right. I just need to take a deep breath. Everything will be fine," she stuttered.

I sighed and parked the car. Getting out, I walked over to Grace and wrapped my arm in hers to remind her that I was there for her. The boys had already gotten us a table and were both waiting with roses for us. Ethan had mine specially made so the rose was blue, my favorite color, while Ryan had a pink rose for Grace. Both of them were so sweet and so romantic. Seeing the rose, Grace's cheeks lit up. She was smiling and blushing to match the rose.

"Hey, sweetie. I love the rose." I smiled while going for kiss from Ethan.

"Hi, Grace. You look lovely tonight," Ryan said before kissing Grace on the cheek.

"Thank you. Denise helped me with the outfit. I hope I'm not too over-dressed," she said shyly.

"Of course not. So why don't we all sit? Then we can order, and Grace can tell us all about the book you two have been reading." Ethan grinned.

Smiles all around, we sat and ordered.

"Well, we have been reading this crazy book about mythical creatures that is still a romance. It's more of Denise's type of book. I'm more into mystery," Grace started.

"No way! You like mystery? I love mystery. Who is your favorite author?" Ryan interjected.

Looking at Ethan, I knew he had set up the perfect conversation for those two. By the end of the night, they would definitely share their first kiss. I was so happy for them, and Ethan knew how I felt. Wrapping his arm around me, I knew there would be many more dates for them. Hopefully, the four of us would share many more dates like this.

Chapter Eighteen

Graduation

Senior year of high school had passed, along with four years of college. Senior year of high school year was one of the most memorable years of my life. I had started a new life myself that year and met the world's greatest best friend, who was also the greatest man alive, aside from the man I sat next to every day, whether it was in the car or on my couch. That man I sat next to was the best part of my new life. We had been together ever since I started my new way of living.

Today, though, was our graduation day. We were all together and graduating to enter our new lives as adults. Ethan, that man I was sitting next to, had a special dinner planned for us tonight. I also knew for a fact that Ryan was going to propose to Grace tomorrow night on her birthday. I was so excited that Ryan even let me help out with picking the ring for her. She was totally in love with him. Just the way I was totally in love with Ethan.

After the ceremony, I met my mom, who was crying and hugging me at the same time. She couldn't believe her twenty-one-year-old daughter was finally out of college and was with someone so special. Both Ethan's family and my mom and I went out to dinner together. Carly, now nine, was looking beautiful and still bouncing off the walls. I knew she knew what Ethan had planned during this dinner, but what I imagined was nothing close to the actual plan.

"Attention, everyone. I would like to give a toast to Denise and me for graduating and for Denise already having job offers from all around. I wanted to make this dinner special, and how else could it be more special than surrounded by our loved ones? Well, I'll tell you how." He smiled and looked at me. His eyes never left as he got down on one knee in front of me, and I almost started crying. "Denise, the only way you could make this dinner any better is if you say yes to marrying me. I want to spend the rest of my life with you. Will you marry me, Denise?"

"YES!" I screamed and hugged and kissed him. "I love you so much, Ethan."

It was the greatest dinner, and I was engaged. Everyone had been in on it, even my mother. I later found out he had asked her, since my father wasn't there, for my hand in marriage. So traditional, but that was what I loved about him. Carly was so excited, she couldn't help but ask over and over if she could be the flower girl.

That night, Ethan drove me home after the celebration dinner of our graduation and engagement. I didn't want him to leave, so he spent the night. Unlike the first time we slept together, he was in my room and bed with me, wrapped in his arms and kissing him. We didn't have sex, but it was still such a wonderful night just sleeping in his arms and waking up to him. All because of him from the very beginning made the past four years amazing and the next fifty to come even more enjoyable. My last words to him that night surprised me but left it as a joke for the years to come.

"I can't believe I became a fiancé on the day of our graduation."

Chapter Nineteen

Happy Ending

It's been twenty years since that dinner. To show for those twenty years, I've been married and had two beautiful children. I'm also a high school English teacher at my son's school. Ethan and I had a beautiful son named Ben, and he is fifteen years old. He has a sister who is seven named Amelia. The two of them are our pride and joy. When we leave them, I know they will do great things with their lives. Having the both of us here to love them is all I ever hoped for in this life of mine. Being forty-one, it seems too early to think about death, but not for Ethan.

Ethan was diagnosed with cancer last month, and nothing seems to help. I'm afraid I will lose him before he can see his children marry. Ben has been the strong one for us all. He helps as often as he can to let Ethan and I have some time together at night at the hospital. Amelia doesn't know how to act and keeps asking if Daddy is going to be okay. I tell her everything will be fine, but in my heart, even I'm scared that it may not.

"Denise, darling, don't worry so much. Ben and Amelia need you, and I'll be fine. Amelia is missing out on those amazing bedtime stories you tell."

Ethan smiled on the night I came to see him. He always smiled when I came to see him, but this night seemed even harder for him to do so. I could see he was in pain, and I knew it might be my last night with him.

"I love you so much, and Ben is doing amazingly. Amelia knows those stories by heart. Amelia made this for you. It's a card to get better soon. We all signed it. We miss you at home. You need to get better. I know you're struggling, but promise you won't stop fighting," I begged.

"My love, I can't keep fighting this. I want to and I miss you and the children, but it's stronger than me, and I've heard the doctors saying there is nothing they can do for me. I will fight for one more day so I can see the kids, but I won't last forever. They need you and you need to be strong for them."

"Ethan, no. Please don't give up. The doctors are wrong. You will be okay. You promised to stay with me."

I was crying and couldn't stop. Tomorrow the children would not be going to school if their father wouldn't fight. I didn't want them to miss any more time with him. I ran out of the room and drove home. Waking up Amelia and Ben, we all went to my room to sleep. Ben, even though he was fifteen, knew I needed him and hugged Amelia and me.

"My strong son, I love you so much," I whispered since Amelia was asleep again.

"We aren't going to school tomorrow, are we, Mom?" Ben asked.

"No. You two are spending the day with your father. He wants to see the both of you and tell you how much he loves you both."

"He is going to die, isn't he?"

"Shh, don't think about that now, just sleep, baby. I want you to smile tomorrow and look upon your father the way you did when you were a boy."

Those were the last words I said before crying silently to sleep. Waking up the next morning, we all piled into the car and drove to the hospital. I let the children spend most of the day with their father, then had my mother come pick them up around dinnertime. I knew he would be letting go soon, and I couldn't leave him.

"I love you, Denise. Amelia looks like you so much, and Ben, when did he get so tall?" Ethan asked.

Watching his face light up, I knew he was trying to distract me.

"Don't say goodbye, Ethan. I don't want to hear you say goodbye ever," I responded.

"Wouldn't dream of it, darling. All I want to say to you is that you stay strong for those kids, just like I know you will. We will see each other again, and I'll be watching over you all."

Before he closed his eyes for the last time, we shared our last kiss. I couldn't leave him or let go of his hand. Ben, who had recently gotten his license when he turned sixteen the week before his father's death, came and picked me up.

I spent the nights crying. Ben had stayed strong and when I looked at him, I saw Ethan's strength. I knew I needed to be the strong one.

The day of Ethan's death was over a month ago. Amelia and Ben are sitting in the other room as I write this story. Ben, who now has a girlfriend, and Amelia, who loves to dance in the sunlight. Carly comes and visits them and me as often as she can. Amelia and Ben, my children, are strong like their father. I see the light I remember in him shine within them. Even though he has left me, I know he will always be in my heart. His death was not the happiest moment of my life with him, but even though he is gone, I'm still the person I am today because of him. I guess sometimes that's all you can ask for—a happy ending.